This book belongs to:

Violet!
On your 6th Birthday!

To my kind and funny Hennie, who makes me laugh and taught me how to play again. I am so proud of you.

Thank you to Clare Thompson, a published author herself, who was so generous with her time and advice.

Thank you to Andrea Mitchell, my proofreader and friend.

To see more of Sue Rinaldi's artwork visit:
www.soobaloo.co.uk

Published in association with Soobaloo Art for Amazon KDP Publishing.

Text copyright ©2020 Susie Brown

Illustrations copyright ©2020 Sue Rinaldi

ISBN: 978-1-5272-8064-9

THE BUTTERFLY

THAT COULDN'T FLY

Written by

Susie Brown

Illustrated by

Sue Rinaldi

Once upon a time there was a little girl called Hennie. Hennie was just four years old and loved wearing cute dresses. Hennie lived in a square house with her Daddy, Mummy and her two baby brothers Rups and Barnaby.

Hennie had her own room with a big window to look out at the pretty flowers, trees and birds in the garden. She had a snugly bed and a bedside table with an alarm clock. When it was time to get up a sun would shine from the alarm clock.

It was Saturday morning and Hennie wriggled in her bed waiting for the sun to come up on her alarm clock. "Come on sun," she said. "I want to get up and do some colouring."

As she said that she heard a tap tap on her window and at almost exactly the same time the sun came up on her alarm clock.

Hennie got out of bed as quickly as she could and opened the curtains. "Oh, look at the beautiful Butterfly sitting on my windowsill," she said. Hennie took a closer look at the Butterfly through her window and the Butterfly looked back at her with tears in its little eyes. Then the Butterfly lifted one of its six tiny legs and tapped on the window.

Hennie carefully opened the window and the beautiful Butterfly slowly walked in. Hennie, who was a very kind girl, opened her hand so that the Butterfly could walk onto it.

Very gently and with great care Hennie carried the Butterfly to her bedside table and let it sit by her alarm clock. Hennie then climbed onto her bed and sat very still and quietly so she could see the Butterfly's face.

"Why are you crying Butterfly?" she asked. The Butterfly looked at Hennie with its little eyes full of tears and said in a very sad voice "it's because I can't fly." "Oh," said Hennie "why can't you fly?" "Because I am too scared," said Butterfly. Hennie didn't really know what to do, so she made a comfy, safe little bed for Butterfly and then went downstairs to have her breakfast and have a think about how she could help her new friend.

Hennie had a lovely day going swimming and playing with her friends, but in truth she couldn't wait until it was bedtime so she could look after Butterfly. She had been thinking about the sad Butterfly all day long.

At last it was bath time ...

... and then bedtime.

"Don't worry Butterfly," she said. "Tomorrow
I am going to take you into the garden and
I can help you practice flying." Butterfly smiled
and felt very happy that he had found such a
kind and gentle friend who was going to help.

Hennie and Butterfly went to sleep. After sleeping for one hour, Butterfly woke up and wondered if Hennie was awake too. Very quietly Butterfly crept onto her pillow and then carefully onto her nose, which he thought was rather a nice place to sit! Hennie's nose felt soft and squishy. Hennie was in a deep sleep, having a lovely dream about eating ice cream.

Suddenly she felt that her nose was a bit itchy and thought she was going to sneeze. Hennie opened her eyes and got a big shock to see Butterfly's eyes looking back at her.

Hennie twitched and wriggled her nose and tried very hard not to sneeze as she didn't want to scare Butterfly. It was no good though, Hennie felt the sneeze tickling her nose so much that she just couldn't stop it.

A a t i

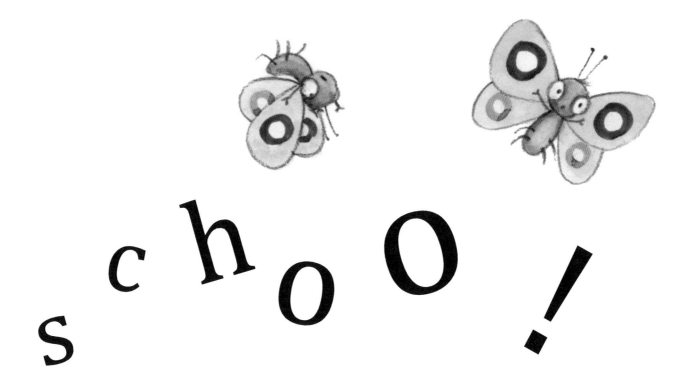

s c h o O !

…went Hennie and Butterfly went flying across the room. Hennie jumped out of bed and saw Butterfly lying on the floor. "Oh no Butterfly," she gasped. "Please be okay."

… But Butterfly was laughing so much that Hennie had to laugh too.

"I can fly, I can fly," laughed Butterfly. "It was such fun and not scary at all!"

Hennie carefully picked Butterfly up and gently put it back beside her bed, next to her alarm clock. "When the sun comes up," said Hennie. "I will open my window and you can fly home."

Morning came and the sun came up on the alarm clock. Hennie opened her window and Butterfly flew outside into her garden with a big smile on its face. Hennie waved goodbye to Butterfly and Butterfly waved goodbye to Hennie with its wings. Hennie knew Butterfly would be very happy flying around in her garden of pretty flowers.

Even to this day, Hennie sometimes hears a gentle tap tap on her window and she knows it's her friend Butterfly who has come to say hello and to thank her for being such a kind and helpful friend.

Why not colour in your own Butterfly?

Printed in Great Britain
by Amazon